Lit'
Pet

ebra
Flowe

CAPSTONE PRESS
a capstone imprint

Little Pebble is published by Capstone Press,
1710 Roe Crest Drive, North Mankato, Minnesota 56003
www.mycapstone.com

Library of Congress Cataloging-in-Publication Data
Clay, Kathryn, author.
 Flowers / by Kathryn Clay.
     pages cm.—(Little pebble. Celebrate spring)
 Summary: "Simple nonfiction text and full-color photographs present flowers in spring"—Provided by the publisher.
 Audience: Ages 5–7.
 Audience: K to grade 3.
 Includes bibliographical references and index.
 ISBN 978-1-4914-8304-6 (library binding)
 ISBN 978-1-4914-8308-4 (paperback)
 ISBN 978-1-4914-8312-1 (ebook pdf)
1. Flowers—Juvenile literature. 2. Spring—Juvenile literature. I. Title.
 QK49.C568 2016
 582.13—dc23   2015023304

Editorial Credits
Erika L. Shores, editor; Juliette Peters and Ashlee Suker, designers;
Svetlana Zhurkin, media researcher; Katy LaVigne, production specialist

Photo Credits
Dreamstime: Jean Schweitzer, 13; Shutterstock: Aksenya, 9, Andrew Mayovskyy, 7, Andrii Koval, 1, Catalin Petolea, 11, Creative Travel Projects, 17, Elena Shutova, 3, green space, 15, honzik7, 21, Nataliiap, cover, Peter Nanista, 19, Ryan Lewandowski, 5, USBFCO, back cover and throughout

Printed in China.   007468LEOS16

Table of Contents

Spring Is Here!

Winter is over.

Spring is here.

We see colorful flowers.

Growing

Rain falls.

The sun shines.

Plants need water
and sunlight.

Stems push up through soil.

Buds start to bloom.

All Kinds of Flowers

Purple petals open.

Jack picks a crocus.

Look on the ground.

Ali spots a daisy.

Look in the tree.

Cherry blossoms grow.

Find a lilac bush.

Its flowers smell sweet.

Look in the yard.

Five tulips grow.

Ella smells red roses.

What flowers do
you see in spring?

Glossary

bloom—to produce a flower

bud—the part of a plant that turns into a leaf or flower

petal—one of the outer parts of a flower

stem—the main body of a plant

Read More

Gleisner, Jenna Lee. *What Blossoms in Spring?* Let's Look at Spring. Ann Arbor, Mich.: Cherry Lake Publishing, 2015.

Rustad, Martha E. H. *Plants in Spring.* All About Spring. North Mankato, Minn.: Capstone Press, 2013.

Smith, Sian. *What Can You See in Spring?* Seasons. Chicago: Capstone Heinemann Library, 2015.

Internet Sites

FactHound offers a safe, fun way to find Internet sites related to this book. All of the sites on FactHound have been researched by our staff.

Here's all you do:
Visit *www.facthound.com*
Type in this code: 9781491483046

Check out projects, games and lots more at
www.capstonekids.com

Index